# SIT STILL!

# BY NANCY CARLSON

**PUFFIN BOOKS**

To Judy—a super teacher who gave me the idea
for this book during a parent-teacher conference,
and
to Pat—who can't SIT STILL!

PUFFIN BOOKS
Published by the Penguin Group
Penguin Putnam Inc., 375 Hudson Street, New York, New York 10014, U.S.A.
Penguin Books Ltd, 27 Wrights Lane, London W8 5TZ, England
Penguin Books Australia Ltd, Ringwood, Victoria, Australia
Penguin Books Canada Ltd, 10 Alcorn Avenue, Toronto, Ontario, Canada M4V 3B2
Penguin Books (N.Z.) Ltd, 182-190 Wairau Road, Auckland 10, New Zealand

Penguin Books Ltd, Registered Offices: Harmondsworth, Middlesex, England

First published in the United States by Viking, a division of Penguin Books USA Inc., 1996
Published in Puffin Books, 1998

1  3  5  7  9  10  8  6  4  2

Copyright © Nancy Carlson, 1996
All rights reserved

THE LIBRARY OF CONGRESS HAS CATALOGED THE VIKING EDITION AS FOLLOWS:
Carlson, Nancy L.
Sit still/by Nancy Carlson. p. cm.
Summary: Patrick has difficulty sitting still until his
mother comes up with a plan to help him.
ISBN 0-670-85721-1
[1. Behavior–Fiction.] I. Title.
PZ7.C21665Si 1996 [E]–dc20 95-46307 CIP AC

Puffin Books ISBN 0-14-056202-8

Printed in the United States of America

**These are chairs.**

Patrick knew 101 different ways to sit in a chair.

Because he knew so many ways to sit in a chair,
he heard two words a lot . . .

**During church Mom would whisper . . . "Sit still."**

**When Dad took Pat out to dinner, he would say . . .**
**"Just sit still and eat."**

On the bus, the driver would yell . . . "Hey kid,
sit still!"

**But it was at school that Pat heard the words**
*sit still* **the most!**

Sit still!

Sit still!

The only class in which he didn't hear "sit still,"
was gym class.

But then again, there were no chairs in gym.

Patrick's teacher got tired of saying "sit still." So she asked his mom to bring him to a special doctor.

Pat made lots of new friends in the doctor's waiting room.

**When it was Pat's turn, the doctor looked in his ears,**

**tested his reflexes,**

and showed him strange pictures.

When the doctor was done he said to Pat's mom,
"I think I know what's wrong.

"Patrick simply can't sit still. There's nothing
more I can do," the doctor said.

Well Pat's mom decided she could do something.
She thought of ways to keep Pat busy.

**She gave him jobs to do.**

She got him a hammer, some nails, and wood.

Instead of trying to sit still in church, Pat joined
the choir.

**Dad and Pat decided that in addition to going out for dinner, they would go bowling each week.**

**Mom and Patrick began walking to school.**

Patrick would get to school early to help the
crossing guard.

When Pat finished his schoolwork, his teachers
gave him special projects to work on.

Nowadays, Pat doesn't have much time for chairs because . . .

he knows 101 things to do *not* sitting still.